FLYING SCOTSMAN
AND THE BEST BIRTHDAY EVER

FLYING SCOTSMAN
AND THE BEST BIRTHDAY EVER

MICHAEL MORPURGO

ILLUSTRATED BY
MICHAEL FOREMAN

T&H

RAILWAY
MUSEUM

My dad was a train driver. But he wasn't just any old train driver. His train was the great Flying Scotsman.

My favourite birthday treat when I was little was to walk with Mum and Dad to King's Cross station in London to see Dad off to work.

We'd stand on platform 10 and watch him patting the side of Flying Scotsman, always the shiniest and most beautiful train in the station.

It was all a wonder to me – to see him climbing up onto
the footplate of the driver's cab, pulling on his driver's
gloves, rubbing down his levers with his cloth, checking
everything all around him.

I dreamed of only one thing – to be up there with
him, to shovel the coal, to pull the whistle, to help him
drive that magnificent giant of an engine.

On each of my birthdays, Mum and I would stand there on the platform, hearing doors slamming and whistles blowing, watching the flag waving and Flying Scotsman like a waking dragon, groaning and grinding into life. The chuffing and chuntering would begin very slowly, the wheels hardly turning at first. But soon enough she would be moving away, wrapped in a cloud of thundering smoke and hissing steam.

To watch my smiling dad waving and calling out to me, 'Happy birthday, Iris!' was the best birthday present in the world. I felt so proud of him.

My only sadness was that I was not going with him.

After we'd seen the train off, I'd have breakfast with Mum
in the station café – some lemonade and a sticky bun with a
candle on it. Then I'd go off into school as happy as you like.

I enjoyed going to school on my birthday, because everyone
sang 'happy birthday' to me in Assembly, and the teachers
and my friends were nicer to me than usual.

It was on my 8th birthday that Mr Merton, our class teacher, asked all of us, one at a time, to make a wish. 'What is it you most wish for in all the world? Iris, your turn first. You're the birthday girl.'

I didn't have to think about it. 'I want to go to King's Cross station, get up onto the driver's footplate on my dad's train, Flying Scotsman, and go all the way with him up to Scotland. It's the fastest train in the whole wide world, sir.'

Mr Merton smiled down at me. 'I know it is, Iris. But I don't think little girls would be allowed up in the driver's cab, even though the driver is your dad. Far too dangerous.'

I lay in bed that night thinking about how unfair it was. Mr Merton didn't tell anyone else they weren't allowed their wishes. Mine was the only wish that he said could never come true.

I asked Mum the next day if I could go with Dad up to Scotland on Flying Scotsman one day soon. I was sure she'd say yes. But she replied: 'No, Iris dear. Maybe when you're older.'

But I wouldn't take no for an answer. I worked it all out, made a plan. And then I did it a few days later.

I wrote a letter the night before. It said:

Dear Mum, gone on the train with Dad. Don't worry, I will be all right. Love from Iris.

It was a windy morning after a stormy night. I had not slept a wink. I lay there in my bed, fully dressed under my blankets. I heard Dad getting up, heard the front door open and shut. I left the letter on my pillow and then I crept out of the house. It was still dark as I followed Dad to the station, keeping a safe distance behind him just in case he looked around. He didn't.

No one was checking tickets on platform 10. I found an open door, climbed in, walked along and found the guard's van, sat down behind some sacks and waited. Easy-peasy. I heard the engine steaming up, felt the train trembling with it. Doors were slamming everywhere. I heard passengers' footsteps out on the platform, heard people talking, laughing. More sacks were thrown into the guard's van. The last sack landed with a thump, the door slammed closed. My hiding place was getting better and better. It was all going so well.

I was sitting there, longing to hear the whistle, to feel the wheels turning, to hear the chuntering and the chuffing. But none of that happened. Nothing happened. The train never moved. For a long while I just sat there.

Suddenly I heard Mum's voice calling me from outside, then Dad's voice too. Moments later, I heard the door open, and then they were inside the guard's van and pulling away the sacks. 'We know you're in here, Iris!' It was Dad. 'Someone saw you getting in.'

I stood up. I had no choice. Mum was not pleased. Dad was not pleased. No one was pleased.

I found out that a tree had ruined my plan. It had come down in the storm the night before on the track just outside the station. So Flying Scotsman had been stuck in the station, unable to leave. Meanwhile, Mum had found my letter, and run all the way to the station. Thanks to the fallen tree, the train was still there, and I never did get to ride with Dad that day on Flying Scotsman.

But then, not long after, something did happen, something wonderful. Dad kept it as a surprise till the last moment. He told Mum and me one evening that we were all going somewhere very special early the next morning. We kept asking what the surprise was, but he wouldn't say.

All Dad said was, 'You'll soon see.'

The next morning, in our very best clothes, we all walked to the station together. Dad went on ahead of us up the platform, until he came to the First Class carriage. Then he told us, 'Today we are going to try to break the speed record on our journey up to Edinburgh, and the railway company asked what gift I'd like to mark the occasion. I said I don't want a watch, nothing like that. I want tickets for my family to travel First Class on Flying Scotsman to Edinburgh.'

Mum was over the moon. I was over the moon.

'They'll look after you like you're royalty,' Dad continued. 'You get on, and I'll go to the driver's cab to get up steam. I'll see you at the other end, when we've broken the record.'

I still couldn't believe it. Mum couldn't believe it.

We looked around us then. Everyone was all
dressed up in their finest, looking very fancy.

We had the best seats in the carriage, window seats, opposite each other, so we could look out all the way to Scotland.

Soon after we left the station, we were invited to breakfast in the restaurant car, served to us by waiters. I'd never had a breakfast like it before or since. We had a proper slap-up lunch later too.

Dad was right – we were treated like royalty. But what I remember best was the rhythm of Flying Scotsman as we raced along, and her whistle as we thundered through stations, and into tunnels.

I was thinking all the while, it was my dad
driving this train, breaking this record.

And out of the window I saw the whole big
wide world passing before me.

The fields and farms, the cows and horses and sheep, the villages
and towns, the castles and churches, the rivers and sometimes
the sea, the hills and valleys, the moors and marshes.

There were some deer, lots of rabbits and
hares ... even a fox once, just sitting there
in a field looking up at us as we roared past.

What a day to remember! My dad drove Flying Scotsman faster than he'd ever driven her before, in fact faster than any train had ever gone before from London to Edinburgh. My dad broke the record.

There was quite a to-do at Waverley station in Edinburgh when we arrived, I can tell you. Flags and bunting flew everywhere, bands played, everyone clapped and cheered. And my dad was the hero. I promised myself there and then that when I grew up, I would work like Dad on the railways.

But that was not easy, not if you were a girl. Women weren't allowed to work on the railways, and certainly not to drive the trains. There was a lot that women weren't allowed to do in those days. Then I got lucky – not that I should call it lucky. When I was in my 20s, the Second World War came, and the men were needed to go and fight in the army or the air force or the navy. So women were needed to work on the railways.

That was how I found myself working in the signal box at King's Cross station. I had my own levers to pull, to change the points and help the trains on their journeys. I can't tell you how many times I sent Flying Scotsman on her way north to Scotland.

She was painted in wartime black now, not bright and shiny green any more, but still the finest train in the world. No other train looked like her. My dad would often be the driver, and he'd wave at me from the footplate of his beloved Flying Scotsman as he passed by.

And when the time came to celebrate the anniversary of Flying Scotsman's record-breaking run to Edinburgh, they asked me as the daughter of the driver to go up to the museum where they still kept her. Wasn't that wonderful! I was a very old lady by then, but I said yes – well, of course I did. The engine was green again and as bright and shining as ever.

But I did make one condition: that they would allow me to climb up onto the footplate of Flying Scotsman, where I'd always dreamed of standing when I was little. And they said yes.

So I stood on that footplate at last. I cut the ribbon, and a band played, and I had a fine old time. No hiding in the guard's van that day! Best moment of my life.

FLYING SCOTSMAN

• FACT FILE •

Flying Scotsman is the most iconic locomotive in the world. She was designed by Sir Nigel Gresley, a leading British steam-locomotive engineer. She was built at Doncaster Works in England in 1923. Flying Scotsman went on to break several world records during her long and illustrious career.

After her retirement in 1963, Flying Scotsman visited the United States, Canada and Australia, gaining fans from around the world. She settled back in the United Kingdom, where she has been carefully restored. Flying Scotsman has been back on the tracks since 2016, taking special passenger tours across the UK.

THE STATS

Name:	Flying Scotsman
Numbers:	1472; 4472; 502; 103; E103; 60103
Builder:	Doncaster Works, England
Build date:	February 1923
Designed by:	Sir Nigel Gresley
Weight:	97 tonnes
Length:	21 m
Height:	4 m
Colour schemes:	Apple green; wartime black; British Railways blue; British Railways green
Career:	Passenger locomotive for London and North Eastern Railway (1923–47) and British Railways (1948–63)
Retired:	1963
Home:	National Railway Museum
Known for being:	Daily traveller from London to Edinburgh; record-breaker; museum exhibit; touring international superstar

Record-breaker

1928: First non-stop run from London to Edinburgh

1934: First steam locomotive to reach 100 mph

1989: Longest non-stop run by a steam locomotive: 680 km!

1989: First steam locomotive to circumnavigate the globe

2016: Oldest mainline working locomotive on tracks in the United Kingdom

Flying Scotsman in the United States and Canada (1969–73)

In 1969, Flying Scotsman arrived in the United States for an ambitious trade promotion tour. To meet with US rail safety regulations, the front of the locomotive had to be fitted with a large headlight, a bell and a cow-catcher.

During this tour, the famous locomotive gained new fans across the United States of America and Canada. Flying Scotsman received a hero's welcome on her arrival home!

Flying Scotsman in Australia (1988–89)

In 1988, Flying Scotsman was invited to visit Australia
as the star attraction in the Aus Steam '88 festival.
Flying Scotsman arrived in Sydney. From there, she
travelled to Melbourne for the exhibition. She went on
to tour across Australia. The year was concluded
with a run from Sydney to Perth via Alice Springs.

Flying Scotsman returned triumphantly to the UK in December 1989. Having visited three continents, she was the first steam locomotive to circumnavigate the globe. Truly the most famous locomotive in the world.

Fun fact:
All locomotives are traditionally referred to as 'she' and 'her' — even trains
with names like Flying Scots*man*!

First published in the United Kingdom in 2022 by
Thames & Hudson Ltd, 181A High Holborn, London WC1V 7QX

Published in association with the National Railway Museum
National Railway Museum logo © SCMG Enterprises Ltd

Flying Scotsman and the Best Birthday Ever is based on historical
events, but the story and its characters are works of fiction. Any
resemblance to actual persons, living or dead, is entirely coincidental.
The real record-breaking driver of Flying Scotsman when it reached
100 mph in 1934 was William (Bill) Sparshatt.

British Library Cataloguing-in-Publication Data
A catalogue record for this book is available from the British Library

ISBN 978-0-500-65294-7

Printed in China by RR Donnelley

Be the first to know about our new releases,
exclusive content and author events by visiting
thamesandhudson.com
thamesandhudsonusa.com
thamesandhudson.com.au